Mad about

Pirates

written by Rupert Matthews
illustrated by Sue Hendra and Paul Linnet

consultant: Bob Rees

A catalogue record for this book is available from the British Library

Published by Ladybird Books Ltd
80 Strand London WC2R 0RL
A Penguin Company

2 4 6 8 10 9 7 5 3 1
© LADYBIRD BOOKS LTD MMVIII
LADYBIRD and the device of a Ladybird are trademarks of Ladybird Books Ltd

Produced by Calcium for Ladybird Books Ltd

ISBN-13: 9781 84646 923 7

Printed in China

Contents

Some words appear in **bold** in this book.
Turn to the glossary to learn about them.

What are pirates?

The word pirate means 'attacker'. Pirates were men, and sometimes women, who captured **merchant ships**. They stole a ship's treasure and **goods**, plus sometimes the ship as well.

Some large merchant ships carried a lot of gold and treasure. Pirates who captured these ships could become very rich, very quickly.

Some merchant ships didn't just carry gold. They were decorated with it, too!

Pirates have been around since people learned to sail boats. There were pirates in Ancient Greece and Roman times. And the Vikings were some of the most famous pirates of all.

Pirates fought fiercely. They could also be very cruel to captured sailors.

Pirate ships

Pirate ships came in many shapes and sizes. Some were big, with over twenty **cannons** and 200 men. Others were small, with just a few guns and a small crew. Small ships were called sloops or cutters.

Large pirate ships attacked big merchant ships carrying many goods. That meant more treasure for the pirates!

large pirate ship

Pirate captains flew frightening flags on their ships. These were used to scare the crews of merchant ships, so they would surrender without a fight. Pirate flags were called 'jolly rogers'.

Stede Bonnet's flag

Henry Avery's flag

Blackbeard's flag

Thomas Tew's flag

If you have a computer, you can download a poster of pirate flags from www.ladybird.com/madabout

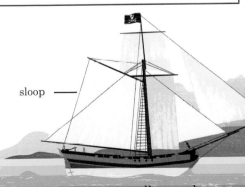

sloop

inlet

Sloops or cutters were small enough to hide in **inlets**, but they could only attack small merchant boats.

9

Life on board

Pirates worked hard on board their ships. They cleaned, cooked and raised and lowered the sails by pulling on ropes.

hat

bandana or head scarf

belt

red waist sash

doublet or coat

breeches or trousers

boots

Pirates did not wear a uniform. They wore whatever they liked. Most pirates wore a jacket, sailor's shirt, trousers and a red sash around their waist.

Pirates sang **shanties** to keep time with each other as they worked.

Pirates took supplies of dried food on their sea trips, because it did not rot. They ate biscuits, dried fish, meat and hard cheese. Sometimes the biscuits had beetles called weevils inside them. Pirates ate them anyway!

weevil

11

Pirate weapons

Pirates usually tried to board a merchant ship, rather than damage it in battle. They fought the crew with swords called **cutlasses** and daggers.

In battle, pirate ships fired **cannonballs** at merchant ships. The balls ripped through sails and **rigging**. The damage to its sails stopped the ship from sailing away.

cannon

12

Pirates used axes to help them climb up a ship's wooden sides.

Spiked pieces of metal shaped like a starfish were thrown onto the deck of a merchant ship. They were called crow's feet and caused terrible injuries if someone trod on them.

Female pirates

Most women only went to sea to be with their sailor husbands. However a few of these women joined pirate crews and became pirates. The most famous female pirates were Anne Bonny and Mary Read.

Women were not usually allowed on pirate ships. They dressed in men's clothes to disguise themselves.

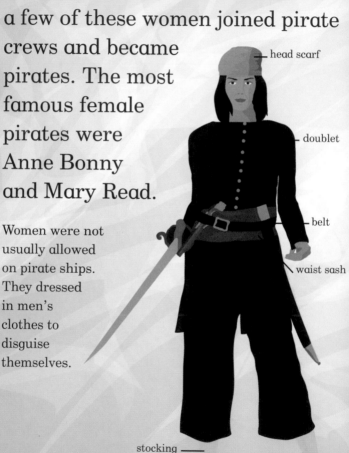

head scarf

doublet

belt

waist sash

stocking

shoe

14

Anne Bonny and Mary Read
fought with a crew run by
pirate captain Jack Rackham.

Jack Rackham

Mary Read

Anne Bonny

Mary and Anne
were eventually
caught by the
British **navy**.
Mary died in
prison, but Anne
was later released.

Pirate treasure

Pirates stole all sorts of things, but gold and treasure were most valuable. Pirates also stole goods such as sacks of rice and sugar, barrels of **molasses** or dried fish, and even cloth. Pirates sold the goods when they sailed into **port**.

Pirates often wore fancy, brightly coloured clothes. They bought them with the money they stole.

Pirates stole any coins they could find. Doubloons were coins made from heavy gold. Pieces of eight were smaller coins made from silver.

doubloons

pieces of eight

Only a few pirates buried their treasure. Most spent it.

Pirate laws

Articles were rules that pirates agreed to before they could join a crew. The rules explained how treasure would be divided up and how pirates should behave. Pirates were punished if they broke the rules – especially if they stole from another pirate.

One punishment was called 'walking the plank'. Pirates were made to jump into the ocean – then the ship sailed away!

Treasure was divided into piles at the end of a trip. Often, a blindfolded pirate chose who got each pile.

Sometimes pirates were left on far-away islands on their own. This punishment was called marooning.

Life ashore

Pirates sailed into ports to find food and water, and to repair their ships. They also sold their treasure in ports. Pirates had to be careful ashore. If they were caught, they could be **arrested** and put on **trial**.

Pirates had fun in ports. They spent the money they made at sea on wild parties, food and drink!

Seaweed and **barnacles** grew on the bottom of pirate ships. They were scraped off the ship while it was ashore.

Madagascar is an island off the coast of Africa. Between 1680 and 1710, it became a pirate island. Pirates set up home there with their families.

Some pirates **gambled** all of their money when they came ashore.

21

A pirate's fate

Some pirates were lucky. They made a lot of money and **retired** to enjoy it. Others were not so fortunate. Some died in battle or were killed by other pirates. If caught, pirates were punished horribly.

Captured pirates were usually hanged. Sometimes their bodies were put in a metal frame as a warning to other pirates. This was known as being hung in irons.

Pirates were often measured to fit their frame before they were hanged.

metal frame

Sometimes, pirates were branded as a punishment. This meant being burned with a hot iron shape, to mark them for life.

pillory

Pillories were wooden boards that held people by their wrists and necks. Pirates were chained to them so people could throw things at them, or call them names.

23

Famous pirates

A few pirates became very famous. Blackbeard is the most famous of all. His real name was Edward Teach, but he was called Blackbeard because he grew a long, black beard and tied it into lots of plaits.

When Blackbeard fought, he lit matches and put them in his hair to make him seem even more frightening!

Edward Low was such a cruel captain that his own crew set him **adrift** in a rowing boat with no food and water!

Ching Shih was the wife of a Chinese pirate captain. When he died, she took control of his crew and became an even greater captain than her husband. Ching Shih ruled 1,800 ships and their crews, and stole treasure from everywhere along the coast of China.

Fantastic facts

- Sometimes pirate ships flew a red flag. The flag told other ships that the pirates would fight to the death and kill everyone on board.

Christopher Moody's flag

- Pirates were not allowed to steal from each other. If they did, their ears and nose were cut off as a punishment.

- A pirate crew could use their captain's cabin whenever they wanted.

- Blackbeard's favourite drink was rum mixed with **gunpowder**!

- Pirate captains paid their crew for any injuries received in battle. A finger or an eye could be worth 100 silver pieces. Some pirates may have been paid 600 silver pieces for an injured leg or arm.

26

- If they didn't like their captain, pirate crews could vote for a new one.

- Each pirate captain designed his own flag.

- Captured pirates were not always hanged. Some were pardoned. That meant their king forgave them.

- Captain Kidd made about two million pounds as a pirate. He was one of the richest pirates.

- **Shipwrecked** or marooned pirates often found very little food on **desert islands**. Rather than starve, they sometimes ate their belongings, or each other!

Amazing pirate awards

Most treasure

In 1695 pirate captain Henry Avery stole all the treasure on board the *Gang-I-Sawai*. It was worth about 140 million pounds in today's money!

Biggest party

In 1718 Blackbeard and his pirate friend Charles Vane threw a party for their crews. It lasted for over a week!

Kindest pirate

Edward England's crew thought he was too kind. They sacked him and left him on a desert island!

Best ship

The *Royal Fortune* was the most powerful pirate ship. It was a **warship** and had 52 guns.

Shortest career

Just one hour after John Eaton became a pirate, he was captured by the navy. He was hanged for being part of a pirate crew.

Youngest pirate

Johnny Bleard became a pirate when he was just 13 years old!

Glossary

adrift – when someone is put in a boat and left at sea.

arrested – to be held in prison for breaking the law.

barnacles – small animals that can glue themselves to rocks and ships.

cannon – a big gun that fires metal balls.

cannonball – a metal ball fired from a cannon.

cutlass – a heavy sword with a short blade.

desert island – an island that no one lives on.

gamble – to bet money, or possessions.

goods – anything that can be bought, such as food, clothes and furniture.

gunpowder – a powder that makes explosions when it is lit.

inlet – where the sea reaches further inland than the rest of the coast.

merchant ship – a ship that carries goods.

molasses – a type of thick, dark syrup.

navy – sailors and ships that work for the king or government of a country.

port – a town next to a harbour.

retire – when someone stops working.

rigging – ropes that hold up masts.

shanty – a song that has a strong rhythm and is used to help people work.

shipwrecked – when a ship is destroyed and the crew are forced to abandon it.

trial – when a court hears how a person has broken the law and decides how they will be punished.

warship – a ship built to fight battles at sea.